THE EVENTFUL HISTORY OF
THREE BLIND MICE

THE OPIE LIBRARY

THE EVENTFUL HISTORY OF
Three Blind Mice

ILLUSTRATED BY

WINSLOW HOMER

Introduction by Maurice Sendak ◆ Afterword by Joseph W. Reed

OXFORD UNIVERSITY PRESS
New York

Oxford University Press
Oxford   New York
Athens Auckland Bangkok Bombay Calcutta Cape Town Dar es Salaam
Delhi Florence Hong Kong Istanbul Karachi Kuala Lumpur Madras Madrid
Melbourne Mexico City Nairobi Paris Singapore Taipei Tokyo Toronto
and associated companies in
Berlin   Ibadan

The text of this book has been adapted from the *Eventful History of Three Little Mice and
How They Became Blind,* published in 1858 by the E. O. Libby and Company of Boston,
Massachusetts, as part of the Good Child's Library. Winslow Homer's illustrations are
reproduced from the original 1858 edition.

The illustrations in this book are from the 1858 edition of the book in the
Betsy Beinecke Shirley Collection of American Children's Literature at the
Beinecke Rare Book and Manuscript Library, Yale University.

Design: Nora Wertz

Library of Congress Cataloging-in-Publication Data

The eventful history of three blind mice / illustrated by Winslow Homer;
introduction by Maurice Sendak; afterword by Joseph W. Reed.
p.   cm. — (The Iona and Peter Opie library of children's literature)
ISBN 0-19-510558-3
[1. Folklore. 2. Nursery rhymes—Adaptations.]
I. Homer, Winslow, 1836–1910, ill. II. Three blind mice. III. Series.
PZ8.1.E955   1996
398.24'5293233—dc20   95-35926
CIP

3 5 7 9 8 6 4 2

Printed in Hong Kong on acid-free paper

INTRODUCTION

This introduction could have been titled "Winslow Homer: His Secret Life as a Children's Book Illustrator." Homer's secret remains very well kept, even from most of his admirers. Unlike many of his fellow painters, who looked to Europe for inspiration, Homer enjoyed a sturdy career as a journeyman artist for American book publishers and weekly pictorial magazines. The full flowering of popular printing techniques in the early 1850s opened the door wide for this talented artist who was eager to learn and to earn a good living. But it was the very peculiar character of Homer's genius that turned potentially ephemeral work into serious art.

As David Tatham points out in his study *Winslow Homer and the Illustrated Book*, between 1855 and 1887 Winslow Homer made more than 160 drawings to illustrate works of prose and poetry that were published in books and periodicals. The superb illustrations that adorned such weeklies as *Ballou's Pictorial*, *Frank Leslie's Illustrated Newspaper*, and *Harper's Weekly* have long been eagerly sought after by collectors and are now extremely difficult to find.

Between 1857 and 1859, Homer did forty-odd illustrations for thirteen books for children. Almost all were products of the American Sunday School movement, which had strict standards dictating their moral purpose and Christian content. These books, printed in limited numbers, are almost completely unknown, and they are of little interest except for Homer's exuberant quirkiness. Certainly, their puritanical Sunday-school texts deprive them of any literary value.

So nothing prepares us for the *Eventful History of Three Little Mice and How They Became Blind*. In 1858, Homer provided seventeen drawings for this book, and these extraordinary images spring gloriously to life, hinting not only of the Homer to come but presaging the picture book as we know it today. These drawings, typically free of sermonizing, reveal a hard new sense of humor and a fresh, confident, breezy style. The anonymous retelling of the traditional nursery rhyme is heavy-handed and flat-footed, though oddly touching, with a conclusion both shocking and wonderful. The book's interest for me was always Homer, but while preparing this introduction I fell a little in love with the story. Homer, I suspect, did too.

The story literally gets away with murder. Rather than making the mice vicious and deserving of punishment, Homer and the anonymous author conspire to win our sympathy for them, thus leaving us totally unprepared for the baleful ending. Here are three endearing characters, Graysey, Frisky, and Longtail (and kindly Mama makes four), who do no more than exercise their natural curiosity and then pay gruesomely for it with their lives. "They were very dutiful and loving little mice and seldom did anything very naughty to make their mother scold them." Not at all unlike the famous little bunnies who might very well have ended up as badly (baked in Mrs. McGregor's pie!), as Beatrix Potter strongly hinted they could. Potter told her story with infinitely more art, but I think she would have approved the rough-and-tough truthfulness of this tale. It plainly accords with her blunt view of what children could and should tolerate. It tells us there is no one to blame here and no lessons to be learned. The curious and hungry mice are doing what comes naturally and the grumpy humans are doing likewise. The fateful collision is a foregone conclusion, a fact of life that contemporary children are all too familiar with. How this subversive little story got past the Sunday School alarm system is unimaginable.

The audacity of the retelling seems to have inspired the illustrator to heights of broad comedy, keen observation of character, tenderness of heart, and even wickedness. What was he thinking when he scattered bottles of wine and spirits throughout his suite of pictures? Homer didn't care a fig, obviously, for the Sunday School movement and its Temperance bias. He is engaged in entertaining children, conveying the spirit of the story with good cheer and no punches pulled. Soon, at age twenty-six, he would begin the work of becoming one of our greatest painters. Can anyone doubt his probable bemusement at our interest in this bit of juvenilia from his apprentice years? How could he know that this tiny work had sparked his genius? He revealed his famous heart and mind in picturing the comical-tragical story of the three unlucky mice. He gave them a fitting requiem. Children, of course, will see that, and if they are kind and patient they will explain it all to their mamas and their papas.

—Maurice Sendak

"Three blind mice.

See how they run.

They all run after the farmer's wife,

She cut off their tails with a carving knife;

Did you ever see such a sight in your life,

As three blind mice."

THE EVENTFUL HISTORY OF
Three Blind Mice

Farmer Grumpy lived way up in the country, in a very large house. He had a barn and many horses, cows, pigs, and hens, which he fed and took care of every day.

Farmer Grumpy was a pretty severe man, but he was only cross and ugly when he found somebody on his farm who did not belong there.

Although the farmer had a very large house, he had no children. Nobody lived with him except his wife and the servant girl, Susan, so there were many rooms that were not occupied. In the walls of this house, in a snug little corner, lived Mrs. Mouse and her three children, Frisky, Graysey, and Longtail. Frisky was the most lively and always getting into mischief; Graysey's fur was a little darker than his brothers', and Longtail had a very long tail. They were very dutiful and loving little mice and seldom did anything very naughty to make their mother scold them. Sometimes, instead of going off to play in the attic or out in the barn, they would stay at home and help their mother by sewing (for she had taught them how). But whenever they went off to romp around and have a good time, poor little Frisky was always getting into trouble. One evening (for you know the Mouse family sleeps almost all day and runs about in the nighttime, when we are all asleep) their mother told them that if they were very careful and came home early, they might go and find something to eat.

"But," she said, "you must not go out of the house, because if I should happen to want you, I will call you."

"No, Mother," said Longtail, "we will only go down into the cellar and will come to you if we hear you call us."

So off they frisked, racing up and down the walls in high glee, and I think it would have made you laugh to see their long whiskers and funny little tails, if you had looked through a crack in the wall to see what was going on in the house.

At last the three little mice reached the cellar and went straight to the closet, because they had been there so many times before that they knew the way very well. But when they got there, they found that the broom which usu-

ally leaned against the wall, and which they used to climb up to the shelf, had been taken away.

"Isn't it too bad, Frisky?" said Graysey. "What are we going to do?" Frisky looked as sad and sorrowful as you can imagine a little mouse could. So they all set to work to think how they would get up to the shelf. At last, just as they were about to give up in despair, Frisky spied a little piece of string on the cellar floor, and he began to dance about.

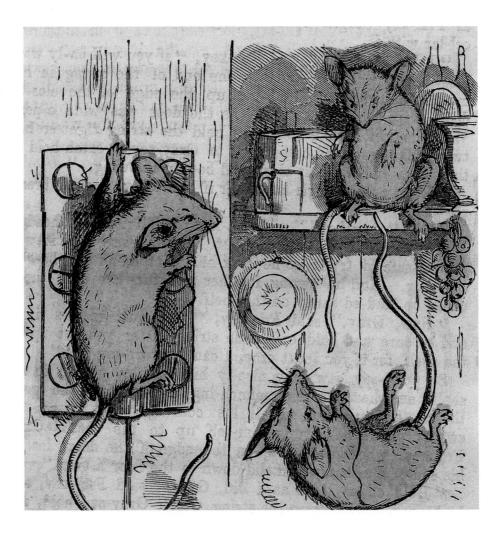

"What are you going to do with that?" asked Longtail, as Frisky took the string and ran all around the cellar with it.

"I will show you," said Frisky, "if you will only wait long enough." So he took one end of the string in his mouth and began climbing up the edge of the closet door, where the hinges were. When he got high enough he held the string tighter between his teeth and called out to Graysey to catch hold of the other end with his claws and begin to swing.

"I am afraid, Frisky. If you let it go I shall break my head."

"Oh! go ahead," said Frisky. "I'll risk your head."

Graysey was still afraid, but Longtail saw that it was pretty safe to try it, so he took hold of the end and began to swing. And he swung further and further each time until he landed safely on the shelf.

"Now, Gray," said Frisky, "you must go this time, and be sure and hold on to the string after you get upon the shelf. If you let it drop, I can't get up myself."

So Graysey saw how nicely his brother got up to the shelf, and hearing him munching and eating the good things, he summoned all his courage and began to swing, until he swung himself up to the shelf. Then Frisky, who was still on the edge of the door, let go of his end of the string and slid down to the floor again.

"Hold on as tight as I did, Gray," said Frisky, and he began climbing up the string that Graysey held, and he was soon with his brothers.

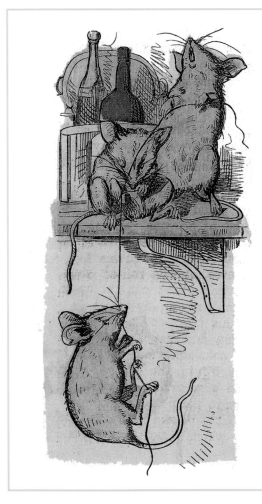

How the farmer's wife would have scolded, if she had seen them eating up her nice mince pies and nibbling the corners of her loaves of bread. There they ate and ate and ate, until they thought that they could eat no more; so Longtail looked at his watch (for he was older than Frisky or Graysey and his mother had given him one) and said it was time to go home. But Frisky was too full of fun and wanted to go out into the barn.

"No, no!" said Longtail, "you know we promised Mother that we would not go out of the house."

"Well, I will only be gone a little while. Besides, it's not half morning yet."

So the naughty Frisky jumped down from the shelf and ran away to the barn, while his more obedient brothers returned to their mother.

"Where is Frisky, my dear children?" she asked, when she saw them coming without their brother. She was very sad when they told her where he had gone. But you will see how he was punished.

Off went Frisky to the barn, whistling as merrily as he could; but he was not very happy, for he knew he was doing wrong.

"O-ho!" Frisky said to himself, "what a fine time I will have among the corn; and I will have it all to myself, too." So he trotted along through the barnyard and went into the barn.

Now, the farmer's horses were all in their stalls, asleep. Frisky thought his little feet would not make enough noise to disturb them; but just as he was passing by Peggy, the farmer's favorite horse, Frisky happened to hit her with the end of his

tail, and Peggy lifted her foot and just grazed poor Frisky's nose, and he rolled over and over.

"Squeek-eeke! Squeeke-eeke!" he cried, as he put his paw up to his nose. He crawled along home, feeling very sorry he had not obeyed his mother. When he got home, his mother did not scold him, because she saw he had been punished for his naughtiness

already; so she put a bandage on his nose and put him to bed. Poor little Frisky was not able to go out with his brothers for some time.

"Ah! those naughty mice," said Susan, the servant, when she went down to the cellar the next morning. "Here are all my pies and bread, bitten and spoiled by those little rascals. I must tell Mrs. Grumpy."

The farmer's wife was very angry when she heard that the mice had been in her closet, and she told Susan that if she ever caught them, she would do something very dreadful, and although Longtail and Graysey were in the wall listening, they could not hear what it was that Mrs. Grumpy said she would do to them, because she whispered it to Susan. I guess they would have been terribly frightened if they had heard what Mrs. Grumpy had said. But they were full of mischief and laughed in their sleeves as they heard the old lady scold.

Under his good mother's nursing, Frisky at last got well. He had gotten so tired of lying in bed that one morning, just as his brothers came home from a little journey, he said to his mother:

"I am going up into some of the big rooms to play a little while in the sunshine." So he kissed his mother and ran off.

Now, I must tell all of you who have read the story of the Three Little Kittens that they lived in this same Farmer Grumpy's house. You will remember that just after they had found their mittens, they saw a little mouse peeping out of his hole. This little mouse was Frisky himself. He had been all over the house and happened to pop up into the very room where Spotty, Whitey, and Blacky were. The moment Frisky saw Spotty coming at him, he jumped and scampered into

his hole as fast as he could. And when he was safely out of the reach of the kittens' paws, he sat down and shook his little sides with laughter.

So Frisky ran home to tell his mother of his adventure.

"Oh! my dear little Frisky," she said, "I'm afraid you will get killed sometime. I believe I shall have to send you to school."

But Frisky thought he knew enough without going to school. Frisky's wonderful escape from the kittens only made him bolder than ever. He would even creep down into the dining room  while Farmer Grumpy and his wife were at supper.

One evening he came running home with some very good news.

"I've been down in the dining room," he said, "and Mrs. Grumpy has made some cheese, which she is going to put into the pantry tonight."

"Hurrah for Frisk!" said Graysey.

"Won't we have a feast!" said Longtail. "Won't you come too, Mother?" he asked, for he was always very thoughtful of his mother.

"No, dear Longtail," she said, "I'm afraid I shall get cold. But you may bring me a piece, and I will toast it at home."

So they waited till they heard Mrs. Grumpy lock the pantry door and saw the old farmer go to bed.

The three little mice were soon in the pantry, eating away at the nice cheese that Mrs. Grumpy had left there. After they had eaten all they wanted, Longtail nibbled and nibbled until he got a piece of cheese that he could tie his tail around.

"Now, Frisk and Gray," he said, "take hold of my tail and pull," and they pulled until a great piece of cheese rolled down on to the shelf.

"What is this great thing?" said Frisky, just as they were all going to leave the pantry.

"Let's find out," said Graysey. So he jumped upon Frisky's back and looked into a great basin of vinegar, which Susan had put there.

"Oh! what a splendid place to fish in," said Graysey. He had never seen any vinegar, and he thought it was water.

"Sure enough," said Frisky, after he had got upon Graysey's back and looked in. "We'll come here and fish."

Then Longtail laid over on his back and took the piece of cheese in his claws, and Graysey and Frisky took hold of his tail and pulled him home, with the cheese for their mother clasped tight between his legs.

"Thank you, my darlings," said Mrs. Mouse, as they set the great piece of cheese before her. "How beautiful it smells. Now take the brush, Longtail, and get yourself clean, and then you had all better go and get some sleep." So she kissed them and told them goodnight.

As they were all going off together, Frisky and Graysey, who had not said anything to Longtail about going fishing, asked him to go with them. The thought of the fun, and a nice breakfast of fish, made Longtail agree to join them.

"But," he said, "what are we going to do for poles?"

"Oh, I'll get them," said Frisky. So he went down into the kitchen and gnawed away at the broom with his little teeth until the floor was quite covered with pieces of it. Then he took the longest and biggest of them and carried them into the pantry. He took thread from his mother's sewing basket to tie to the pieces of broom.

"Hurrah," cried Frisky, as he mounted the edge of the basin.

"Hurrah," cried Graysey, as he followed his brother.

"Hurrah," said Longtail, as Frisky and Graysey helped him up by their side, and they made such a noise that they were frightened that they would wake up Farmer Grumpy and his wife.

"Now we will hold hands," said Frisky, "so we won't tumble in."

"Here we go! here we go!" shouted Graysey, as he tried to throw his thread into the basin, and sure enough they did go, for Graysey gave such a jerk that he lost his balance and fell right into the basin. And he pulled Frisky in, and Frisky pulled Longtail in.

"Squeek-eeke! Squeek-eeke. Oh! Oh, my eyes! Oh, dear me! Oh, what water this is! Squeek-eeke-eeke!" they all screamed together.

"Oh! Frisky! Frisky! what made you come here?" said Longtail, while he was swimming about in the vinegar. "Oh! Squeek-eek-eeke! Oh! how my eyes hurt! Oh, dear! I can't see."

"Nor I," sobbed Graysey.

"Nor I, either," said Frisky. "Squeek! Squeek-eeke! Oh, how shall we get out?"

At last Longtail got his claws on the edge of the basin and Frisky caught hold of his tail, and Graysey got hold of Frisky's tail. So Longtail drew them out. Such

sad-looking creatures as they were, you cannot imagine, all dripping with vinegar and stone blind.

Poor little mice! How they screamed and screamed, and ran about the pantry to find their hole, but they could not see where it was! There they stayed all night, and in the morning, when Mrs. Grumpy went to get breakfast, she took her carving knife and went to the pantry to cut some bread.

"I wonder what all this noise is, in here," so she unlocked the door, and there were the three poor little mice. They could not see, so they ran about, squeaking terribly.

"Three blind mice.

See how they run.

They all run after the farmer's wife,

She cut off their tails with a carving knife;

Did you ever see such a sight in your life,

As three blind mice."

"These are the little rascals I have been hunting for," said Mrs. Grumpy. So she caught poor little Frisky and cut off his tail, and called "Blacky! Blacky!" and Blacky came and swallowed poor Frisky. Then she caught Graysey and cut off his tail and called "Whitey! Whitey!" and Whitey came and swallowed poor Graysey. Then she caught Longtail and cut off his tail and called

"Spotty! Spotty!" and Spotty came and swallowed poor Longtail. Then Mrs. Grumpy took their little tails and laid them by the hole where the three little mice used to come in.

And when their poor mother went to their beds to find them, she saw they were not there. Then she ran down to the pantry, and when she saw their little tails in front of the hole, she ran away from the house, and the cat and her three kittens followed her, full chase, and they were never seen again.

AFTERWORD
Winslow Homer Telling Stories

Winslow Homer's main subjects are Americana and the nostalgic memory of our origins: children at play, one-room schoolhouses, croquet matches in the brilliant light of late afternoon. That these are not true memories for many Americans—and were by no means true for Homer himself—matters much less than Americans' preferred ways of seeing themselves, of patching together the brightly colored images of their lives. Homer painted not just reassuring American wish fulfillment; he was also the premier painter of our greatest national agony, the Civil War. The force and brilliancy of these images—some of them complex in composition and mysteriously allegorical—prompt many historians to count Homer as America's definitive painter, perhaps the greatest in our history.

Yet this high-powered painter of myths began as a craftsman determined to make correct, recognizable figures. This illustrator's power to get the figure right and to tell stories with pictures, Homer's first artistic skills, remained a central feature of his aesthetic.

Winslow Homer's forebears were in America in the 17th century. He was born in Boston on February 24, 1836, and spent much of his life there. His father, Charles Savage Homer, was an importer of hardware. His mother, Henrietta Maria Benson, was a painter, not what you could call an artist, but she made pictures—birds and flowers—all the time, throughout her life. She surely influenced her son's remarkably early determination to draw. "When we moved to Cambridge the idea was to give us boys an education," one of his brothers wrote, "but I was the only one that wiggled through Harvard College. Win wanted to draw."

His father apprenticed Winslow at the age of 18 to John H. Bufford, a lithographer. He was already so skilled at drawing that the $300 fee normally paid to the master was in his case reduced to $100. During this period, he and some other apprentices went to a picture gallery. When Homer said, "I am going to paint," one of the other apprentices, indicating a painting by the French romantic artist Edouard Frère, asked, "Like that?" Homer said, "Something like that, only a damned sight better."

Homer thought making pictures would be a respectable profession. Fortunately, he never thought (as we sometimes do now) that representational pictures were "mere" illustration. But he was not yet a painter; he had to make a living while he found out how to paint. In June 1857 he went to work (he called it "slavery" because it was drawing to order and the hours were long) for *Ballou's Pictorial Drawing-Room*

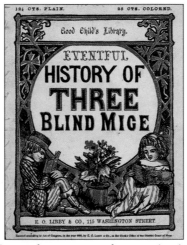

12½ CTS. PLAIN.   25 CTS. COLORED.

Good Child's Library.

EVENTFUL
HISTORY OF
THREE
BLIND MICE

E. O. LIBBY & CO., 115 WASHINGTON STREET.

Entered according to Act of Congress, in the year 1861, by E. O. Libby & Co., in the Clerk's Office of the District Court of Mass.

Companion, a weekly magazine. In August he started to make drawings for *Harper's Weekly*, the foremost periodical of the day. Two years later he left *Ballou's* but continued to accept free-lance assignments for *Harper's*; he had left his apprenticeship and begun his independent career. Drawing for magazine cuts (a skilled artisan would make the actual woodblock used for printing) was his "money crop" and he pursued it aggressively; it

became so useful and profitable that he kept it up as a sideline until 1896, long after he could have supported himself by painting alone.

As he continued to make drawings for magazine cuts, Homer developed skill in action drawing, rendering, shading, and formal composition. He kept up this work not just because he was afraid to stop, but because in working on cuts for *Harper's Weekly* he found discipline. Making the drawings lively gave him a knack for the fine points of visual rendering and narrative. He soon made pictures that told more than they showed. And the best of Winslow Homer's works are, to the end of his career, narrative pictures, visual equivalents of stories.

He drew local color (*A Boston Watering-Cart*) and he illustrated short stories (such as "The Parsonage," published in *Galaxy*, a fiction magazine), novels (*Bessie Grant's Treasure*, published in 1860), and poems (Longfellow's "Excelsior"). He did covers for sheet music (*The Ratcatcher's Daughter*, 1855; *Roger's Quickstep*, 1856). And he did illustrations for 13 children's books—just a few drawings for most of the titles but a full set for one: *The Eventful History of Three Blind Mice*.

Published early in 1858 as part of the Good Child's Library of E. O. Libby & Co., Boston, this 24-page book contains 17 drawings by Homer. (Only the frontispiece is signed, but all are accepted as Homer's work.) David Tatham, in *Winslow Homer and the Illustrated Book*, suggests that he had a British prototype before him, the *Remarkable History of Five Little Pigs*, issued by the firm of Brown, Taggard and Chase in The Good Little Pig's Library. In any event, the book was sold by Libby for "12 ½ cts. plain, 25 cts. colored." The author of the text is unknown, and perhaps that is fortuitous. The text is less powerful than the pictures: this book moves forward by the authority of its pictures.

Homer also provided illustrations for many other texts, true and fictional. For each of these jobs he got a flat fee; he worked with a variety of publishers because he valued his freedom. His work at *Harper's* continued. When the Civil War began, Homer started drawing soldiers in camp. He was issued two official passes during the war, so he almost certainly followed the Union army, but it is not certain he ever witnessed action or that he drew subjects in the field of battle. During this period he began to paint in earnest (he took lessons in Brooklyn). He first turned out paintings that were extensions of his magazine woodcuts; he painted what he drew. Of one such painting, *Sharpshooter* (ca. 1862), Homer

said, "It is about as beautiful and interesting as the buttons on a barn door." But it was a start. These paintings sold well and fetched higher and higher prices. Official recognition was not long in coming: Homer was elected an associate of the National Academy of Design in 1864 and a full member in 1866, at the age of 30.

In the same year, he had his first important public success: *Prisoners from the Front*, a Civil War painting completed after the fighting had ended. It was one of two pictures Homer submitted to the International Exposition in Paris in 1867, and it established him as an artist of international stature.

Homer followed this success as a wartime painter with still greater success as a painter of American genre scenes: images of well-heeled Americans, young and old, working and playing. Sojourns at Tynemouth, England (*A Voice from the Cliffs*, 1882), Gloucester, Massachusetts (*Girl with Laurel*, 1879), and the Adirondack Mountains of New York State (*A Summer Evening*, 1890) gave him fresh material and gave his visual narratives extra depth. Visits to Florida and the Bahamas added new colors to his palette.

Homer worked hard to acquire his reputation as a painter. For the most part he did so without patrons or commissions. But it took the art establishment some time to adjust to his way of looking, simplifying, telling—time to make sense of Homer's remarkable technical mastery of watercol-

or and oils. He seemed to use both so offhandedly; he never claimed mastery, but he had it, and he used spectacular, tour-de-force painting to render unidentified people without beautifying them. His most frequent subject is the human form set against a landscape, much as in William Wordsworth's poetry; like Wordsworth's, Homer's people take on rich meaning through suggestion, contrast, and the expression of the artist's deep feeling.

But Homer never spelled out this meaning. After an exhibition of *The Gulf Stream* (an oil that many think is his greatest painting), M. Knoedler & Co., his dealer, was having trouble answering questions about the painting. Homer replied:

> You ask me for a full description of my picture of the "Gulf Stream." I regret very much that I have painted a picture that requires any description. The subject of this picture is comprised in its title....The boat & sharks are outside matters of very little consequence. They have been blown out to sea by a hurricane. You can tell these ladies that the unfortunate negro who now is so dazed & parboiled, will be rescued & returned to his friends and home, & ever after live happily.

Homer resisted the artist's prerogative to embroider the visual with literary decoration: he thought it unnecessary and dishonest. He had no patience with explanations. As Henry James wrote in *Galaxy*, Homer's paintings "imply no explanatory sonnets."

The artist had neither wife nor children. In 1883 he moved with his brothers and other members of the family to Prout's Neck, a tiny peninsula on the coast of Maine. Later he built a painting shack on the dunes, living apart from his relatives, trying to avoid interruptions. He knew that life was short and art was not, so he painted to the exclusion of all else, in his final years solidifying a vision and a coherent body of work that would not be understood for years. It was a happy and industrious life, and it changed American painting for good.

Homer died at Prout's Neck on September 29, 1910. After his death, his paintings found their way into major museum collections throughout the United States. Over the following century his work became perhaps too well known, almost taken for granted, as familiar as calendar art. Today he is recognized as a major contributor to the development of American painting and to the history of journalistic and fictional illustration. Homer's illustrations for *The Eventful History of Three Blind Mice* are early evidence of his ability to convey motivation and action in two-dimensional rendering. Indeed, whether drawing for woodcuts or painting, whether portraying mice or men, Homer was a master.

—Joseph W. Reed

WINSLOW HOMER (1836-1910) began his career in Boston, where he worked as an apprentice lithographer and illustrator. During the Civil War he won international acclaim for his work as a battlefield correspondent for *Harper's Weekly*. He also provided illustrations for many other popular magazines of the time and for novels, sheet music covers, and 13 children's books. He is best known for his watercolors, and his stunning interpretations of the sea hold a unique place in the history of American art. Homer's achievement is the subject of a major retrospective exhibition at the National Gallery in Washington, D.C., the Museum of Fine Arts in Boston, and the Metropolitan Museum of Art in New York in 1995-96.

MAURICE SENDAK has illustrated more than 80 books for children, including *Where the Wild Things Are*, *In the Night Kitchen*, and *Outside Over There*. For more than 40 years his books have entertained children and adults alike, challenging established ideas about what children's literature is and should be. He has received many honors and awards, including the American Book Award, the Caldecott Medal, and the Laura Ingalls Wilder Medal from the American Library Association.

JOSEPH W. REED is professor of English and American studies at Wesleyan University. He is the author of *Three American Originals: John Ford, William Faulkner, and Charles Ives* and *American Scenarios: The Uses of Film Genre*. Professor Reed is also an accomplished artist whose drawings and paintings have been exhibited in group and one-man shows from Washington, D.C., to New Delhi.

THE IONA AND PETER OPIE LIBRARY OF CHILDREN'S LITERATURE

The Opie Library brings to a new generation an exceptional selection of children's literature, ranging from facsimiles and new editions of classic works to lost or forgotten treasures—some never before published—by eminent authors and illustrators. The series honors Iona and Peter Opie, the distinguished scholars and collectors of children's literature, continuing their lifelong mission to seek out and preserve the very best books for children.

ROBERT G. O'MEALLY, GENERAL EDITOR